SHENANDOAH NOAH

Holt, Rinehart and Winston | New York

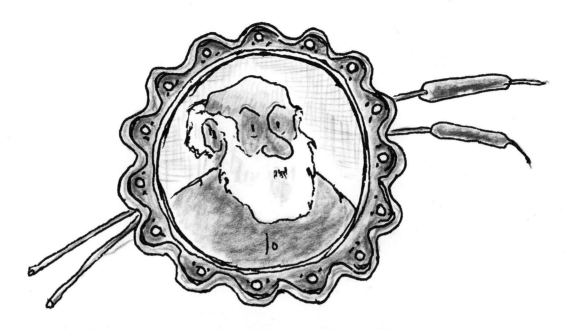

SHENANDOAH NOAH

By JIM AYLESWORTH

Illustrated by GLEN ROUNDS

Text copyright © 1985 by Jim Aylesworth
Illustrations copyright © 1985 by Glen Rounds
All rights reserved, including the right to reproduce
this book or portions thereof in any form.
Published by Holt, Rinehart and Winston,
383 Madison Avenue, New York, New York 10017.
Published simultaneously in Canada by Holt, Rinehart
and Winston of Canada, Limited.

Library of Congress Cataloging in Publication Data
Aylesworth, Jim.
    Shenandoah Noah.
    Summary: Shenandoah Noah's reputation for laziness
gets him into trouble when he catches fleas from his
hounds and decides he has to take a bath.
    1. Children's stories, American.   [1. Mountain life—
Fiction.   2. Humorous stories]   I. Rounds, Glen,
1906–   ill.   II. Title.
PZ7.A983Sh   1985   [E]   84-22554

ISBN: 0-03-003749-2

First Edition

Printed in the United States of America
10 9 8 7 6 5 4 3 2 1

ISBN 0-03-003749-2

To the old wolf himself, Glen Rounds,
from one of his pups.

—J. A.

The artist respectfully dedicates
these magnificent drawings
to Elizabeth Anne [B-HI],
who is well acquainted with Noah
and his mountains.

—G. R.

All his kin are farmers in the valley, but Shenandoah Noah doesn't like farming. Farming means plowing, and plowing means walking behind a mule in the hot sun, and walking behind a mule in the hot sun means work, and work is something that Shenandoah Noah doesn't care for.

Noah likes it much better up in the mountains, where he can live alone with his hounds, and stay happy just sitting in the shade. There was one time, however, that just sitting in the shade wouldn't do at all.

That was the day Noah caught a case of fleas from those hounds. That day, he was jumping and scratching like fury. Even worse, he knew that if he didn't want to scratch his hide off . . .

. . . he'd have to wash himself and all his clothes, and washing is something else Noah doesn't like. Washing means lots of hot water, and lots of hot water means a big fire, and a big fire means sawing and splitting wood, and sawing and splitting wood means work, and work is something Noah doesn't care for.

This time, though, he didn't have a choice. So he sawed
and split some wood and built a big fire.

Then he hauled water to the black pot . . .

. . . dumped in all his clothes and blankets, and stirred and poked them with a stick until they were clean.

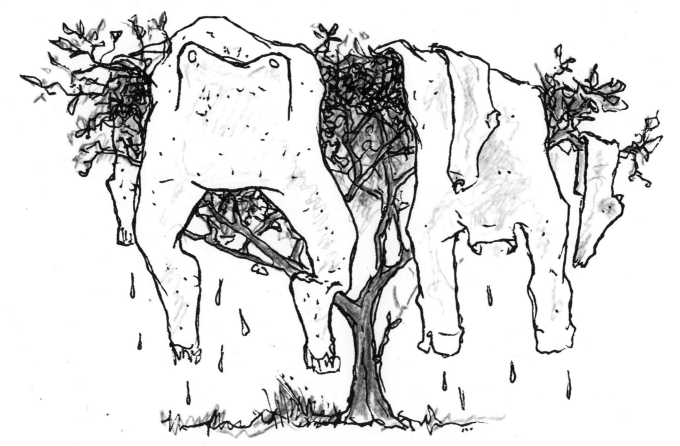

When he was done, he wrung them out and hung them up to dry.

In the meantime, the smoke from Noah's wash fire was making his kin in the valley mighty curious. They weren't used to seeing much smoke coming from Noah's place.

Smoke all morning means a big fire, and a big fire means sawing and splitting wood, and sawing and splitting wood means work, and everybody knew that work is something Noah doesn't care for. Something had to be wrong.

So Noah's nephew Johnny, the biggest of the boys, took the shotgun, and started up the mountain to check on things.

When he got within earshot, Johnny called out, "Uncle Noah! Uncle Noah!"

By then, Noah was busy scrubbing himself in the old washtub.

And being sort of shy and not used to getting much company, he wasn't a bit happy about having any visitors, especially when he looked so silly with his beard full of soap bubbles. So when he heard Johnny calling, he jumped up and ran inside.

And since all his clothes and blankets were wet and hanging in the yard, he lay down on the bed, and covered himself with the bearskin rug.

Johnny came on into the yard and called again, "Uncle Noah! Uncle Noah!" Noah didn't move and didn't say anything.

Then Johnny came up onto the porch and peeked inside.
"Uncle Noah, you in here?"

It was dark in there, and Johnny couldn't see much at first. But when he stepped through the door, he suddenly made out what he thought was a bear lying on Noah's bed.

Johnny was so startled that he jumped backward, tangled up his feet, tripped over a stool, and fell down. When he hit the floor, the shotgun went off—*Ka-Blaam!*—and blasted a hole right through the roof.

The noise scared Noah so bad that he rose up under that bearskin rug, and hollered, "Don't shoot! It's me!"

And when Johnny heard Noah's voice coming from that
bear on the bed, he scrambled out across the porch,

and back on down the mountain just as fast as he could go.

He told everyone in the valley that Noah had turned into a talking bear.

The story made quite a stir for a while. And even though nobody claimed to believe it, everybody was always a little too busy to climb back up there to see if it was true or not.

Of course, that doesn't bother Shenandoah Noah any. He likes being left alone. And in spite of everything, the experience didn't change him any. In fact, it just proved he shouldn't do much else but sit in the shade.

He hasn't even fixed that hole in the roof. Roof fixing means nailing shingles, and nailing shingles means ladder climbing, and ladder climbing means work, and everybody knows that work is something Noah just doesn't care for.

Born in Jacksonville, Florida, **Jim Aylesworth** attended Tulane University and received his B.A. in English from Miami University of Ohio. Subsequently, he received an M.A. from Concordia Teachers College in Illinois. He is the author of several children's books, including *Hush Up!* and *Mary's Mirror*, previously published by Holt. But of all his accomplishments he is most proud of the fifteen years he has spent as a first-grade teacher, where he has learned how much children love to read and to be read to. Mr. Aylesworth currently lives with his family in Hinsdale, Illinois.

Glen Rounds has enjoyed a wide variety of occupations and is the popular author and/or illustrator of numerous children's books, including *Hush Up!*, written by Jim Aylesworth. Mr. Rounds lives in Southern Pines, North Carolina.